GLIMPSE THE
✦ FUTURE ✦

WELCOME TO
PECULIAR,
PENNSYLVANIA!
A PERFECTLY NICE AND
NOT-AT-ALL CREEPY PLACE TO LIVE

ALSO BY LUNA GRAVES
Double, Double, Twins and Trouble
Thriller Night
Monstrous Matchmakers

WITCHES OF PECULIAR

GLIMPSE THE FUTURE

LUNA GRAVES

ALADDIN

NEW YORK   LONDON   TORONTO   SYDNEY   NEW DELHI

ALADDIN
An imprint of Simon & Schuster Children's Publishing Division
1230 Avenue of the Americas, New York, New York 10020
First Aladdin paperback edition March 2023
Text copyright © 2023 by Simon & Schuster, Inc.
Illustrations copyright © 2023 by Laura Catrinella
Also available in an Aladdin hardcover edition.
All rights reserved, including the right of reproduction in whole or in part in any form.
ALADDIN and related logo are registered trademarks of Simon & Schuster, Inc.
For information about special discounts for bulk purchases,
please contact Simon & Schuster Special Sales at 1-866-506-1949
or business@simonandschuster.com.
The Simon & Schuster Speakers Bureau can bring authors to
your live event. For more information or to book an event contact
the Simon & Schuster Speakers Bureau at 1-866-248-3049 or visit our
website at www.simonspeakers.com.
Book designed by Heather Palisi
The text of this book was set in Really No. 2.
Manufactured in the United States of America 0223 OFF
2 4 6 8 10 9 7 5 3 1
CIP data for this book is available from the Library of Congress.
ISBN 9781665906296 (hc)
ISBN 9781665914291 (pbk)
ISBN 9781665906302 (ebook)

GLIMPSE THE FUTURE

CHAPTER 1

In Peculiar, Pennsylvania, it is common knowledge among monsters and humans alike that the best place to get a milkshake any day of the week is Scary Good Shakes. The diner, located at 16 Main Street, has been operating since the 1980s, when a witch named Beatrice Wednesday bought the empty building a few blocks down from Ant and Ron's pharmacy and transformed it into the town's premiere destination for frozen desserts.

Nobody knows whether it's a spell that makes Beatrice's milkshakes so tasty or whether she simply has a way with a blender. In all her years running Scary Good Shakes, she has never shared her secret recipe, no matter how big the bribe or pleading the puppy-dog eyes may be. This bothers some people, especially her competitors, but it has never bothered Dee Maleficent. She thinks—she *knows*—that Beatrice makes the best strawberry shakes in the entire universe, and that's good enough for her.

It's a drizzly Saturday morning and Dee is seated in the back of her dads' van, daydreaming about one of Beatrice's strawberry milkshakes with hot fudge on top. She looks out the window, past the raindrops, where she can see a house with a sign posted in the front window that reads LET'S GO PPS PORCUPINES! Behind the house, in the distance, she sees YIKESSS up on the hill.

Principal Koffin's tower ascends into thick fog that, to Dee, looks a lot like whipped cream. A grumbling sound comes from her stomach.

"I'm *starving*," she says. "I might have to order two milkshakes when we get there."

"You're going to turn into a milkshake," Ron replies, smiling at his daughter through the rearview mirror. "How about some scrambled eggs too?"

"I still can't believe Scary Good Shakes serves breakfast now," Bella says, scrolling on her pink eyephone in the middle seat next to Dee. She shows her screen to Charlie, who's seated on her other side, and they both giggle.

"The perfect end to a totally wicked sleep-over!" Eugene remarks from the row of seats all the way in the back. He and Charlie spent the night at Bella and Dee's house, where they cooked homemade pizzas, coordinated and filmed an elaborate skit to post on Bella's WitchStitch account, and had a *Space Wars* movie marathon.

Eugene grips the headrest in front of him and bounces eagerly in his seat. "Man, I have no idea *what* I'm going to order. Do I go savory or sweet? Do I get a side of hash browns, bacon, or toast? Or do I get *french* toast?"

"You sure you're not a werewolf?" Ron jokes from behind the wheel, as Eugene certainly has the appetite of one.

"You can order as much food as you want, Eugene." Antony smiles at him from the passenger seat. He's wearing his human makeup. "I've heard the pancakes are delicious."

"Who knew Beatrice could make delicious pancakes, too?" Dee says, still looking out the window as they turn onto Main Street. She's thinking maybe she'll order some strawberry pancakes to go with her strawberry shake.

"Oh, I forgot to tell you: Beatrice retired," Ant says. "A new family owns Scary Good Shakes now."

Dee's shriek is so earsplitting that Ron slams on the brakes and yells, "WHAT HAPPENED?"

The driver in the car behind them honks their horn.

"Donna!" Ant's left arm is extended out to the side, a reflex to want to protect them all. "What have we said about overreacting when Pop is trying to concentrate?" He regains his composure and says to Ron, "Go, hon. That horn is giving me a headache."

"Overreacting?" Dee's face is a mix of shock and horror. "I'm never going to have another one of Beatrice's strawberry milkshakes *ever* again and you think I'm *overreacting*?"

"Yes," Bella says, not even bothering to glance up from her phone.

"Come on, Dee, you can't be that surprised," Eugene says. "The woman was ancient even when I was a baby."

"So what?" Dee says, and her tone comes out sharper than she intends it to. "That doesn't mean anything. Witches can live for a long time."

"Maybe she gave the new owners her secret recipe," Charlie says optimistically. "She knows how much her milkshakes mean to the town."

Dee says nothing. She crosses her arms and turns away.

The eye on Bella's phone closes, and she puts it down on her lap. "So who are the new owners, anyway?"

"The Nelson-Pans," Ron says. "A husband and wife with two kids. They moved to town a few weeks ago. Dad and I met them last week and told them about the PSBS. They're excited for the next meeting."

Ant and Ron have been members of the PSBS, or Peculiar Small Business Society, for nearly a decade. Any small business owner in town, human or monster, is invited to join.

"Are they witches like Beatrice?" Bella asks.

Ron and Ant exchange a wary glance.

"They're humans," Ant says. He turns to look directly at Bella. "But they're perfectly fine people, so you be nice. I mean it, Bella Boo."

"In case you haven't noticed, Dad, I'm not the one you need to worry about." Bella scoffs.

She gestures to Dee, who's still staring out the window. The gloomy weather now properly reflects her mood.

There's an empty space right in front of Scary Good Shakes, and Ron parallel parks the car into it. Dee gets out of the car and stands there for a moment, observing the place. From the outside, nothing has changed. The same bubblegum-pink paint coats the building's exterior, the same neon sign lights up the front window. The sight of it makes Dee's heart ache with longing. If only she had known when she got that strawberry shake after school on Monday that it would be her last! She would have savored it more.

"Jeepers creepers." Bella shakes her head, watching Dee sulk. She grabs her sister's arm and pulls her toward the door.

Inside, nearly every table is full, and the room swells with chatter and laughter. It's by far the busiest Bella and Dee have ever seen it. The decor remains largely unchanged except for one detail: The milkshake machine, which used to be on display behind the bar, has been removed. In its place is an open window that connects to the kitchen. The others in the group don't bat an eye, but Dee, of course, notices right away.

"Bella!" she whispers, tugging on her sister's sleeve. "Look, it's so horrible!"

But Bella isn't looking behind the bar. Her attention is fixed on a man sitting alone in a booth. He seems familiar.

"Is that Principal Pleasant?" Bella whispers to her friends.

Dee is half listening, still trying to locate the missing milkshake machine. "Who?"

"The PPS principal." Charlie peeks over Bella's shoulder, trying to get a better look without being too obvious. "I think it is. What's he doing all by himself?"

"Table for six?" the host cuts in, like she's in a hurry. The group follows her down the aisle toward a U-shaped booth at the back of

8

the room. As they pass by Principal Pleasant's booth, he looks up from the big piece of paper he's reading—a map?—and locks eyes with Bella. After a split second of surprise, he smiles wide, putting his large, too-white teeth on full display. The sight is just as unsettling as she remembers.

"Ah, Bella Maleficent," he says cheerfully, quickly flipping over the piece of paper—a little *too* quickly, Bella and Dee both notice. "I told you we'd meet again!"

"Principal Pleasant," Bella says, and it comes out almost like a question. She doesn't remember ever telling him her name. "Nice to see you." Only Dee hears the sprinkle of suspicion in her sister's voice.

"Yes, great to see you all." The principal extends his smile to the rest of the group, making an extra effort to nod at Ron and Antony. "By the way, I'll be in to pick up that prescription later today. My apologies for letting it sit so long. I've been swamped with work."

"Not a problem," Ron says. "Just a reminder that we do have a maximum thirty-day hold policy."

"Understood." The principal nods once. Then he smiles at the kids again. Up this close, Bella notices the stubble on his jaw, the red veins that line the whites of his eyes. "Well, enjoy your breakfast. The banana pancakes are simply to die for."

Bella and Dee smile warily back. There's nothing on the principal's table but the mysterious paper and a nearly empty coffee cup.

The group walks to the back, where their host, a teenage girl, waits by the booth, looking irritated. They settle in and she hurriedly passes out the menus, then walks away without a word. Eugene watches her go with a smitten smile on his face.

"Wow," he says, leaning forward and resting his chin in his hands. "Who is *that*?"

Bella follows his gaze and then furrows her brow. "You mean Miss Miserable? Oh yeah, she seems like a real cup of witch's brew."

"Look, Dee," Charlie says, pointing to the top right corner of the menu. "They still have strawberry milkshakes, plus a bunch of other different flavors."

Dee, slouched into the back of the booth, doesn't smile. "They're not Beatrice's milk-shakes."

"All right, that's enough sulking," Ant says to Dee across the table. "Don't knock it until you try it, as the humans say." He opens the menu, then closes it just as quickly. "You know what, I don't even need the menu. I'm going to see what all the fuss is about with these pancakes. Gretchen was absolutely raving about them at the Creepy Council meeting last night."

The grumpy hostess-slash-waitress appears again. When she speaks, she has about as much enthusiasm as somebody going in for a root canal. "Are you ready to order?"

"No," Bella says, like it's obvious. "We've barely had time to look at the menu."

"What do you recommend?" Ron asks, while Ant shoots Bella a warning look for her snappy attitude. "We've heard great things about the pancakes."

"Yep" is all the waitress says. A moment of awkward silence ensues.

"Well, okay, then." Ron claps his hands together, breaking the tension. "Hands up if you want the pancakes."

Everyone puts their hands in the air except for Charlie, who asks for an order of scrambled eggs and bacon. Then Eugene says, "I'll have that too, plus the pancakes, and home fries, *and* a vanilla shake." The waitress scribbles down their orders on her notepad.

"Dee." Bella nudges her sister. "Don't you want a strawberry shake?"

Dee shrugs. "I guess so." She doesn't look up from her lap.

Bella rolls her eyes. She turns to the waitress and says, "Make that two."

The waitress finishes jotting down their

order, collects the menus, and then moves behind the bar to hang the order slip above the window that connects to the kitchen. Eugene, once again, follows her every move with his eyes.

"Hey, look," he says, pointing at the window.

Bella groans. "We get it. You think she's creepy."

"Not that," he says, though he doesn't meet Bella's eye. "There's a kid working in the kitchen."

Eugene's friends scoot toward him and crane their necks to get a better look. It's true: a boy is standing over the griddle with a spatula in his hand, flipping pancakes.

"*He's* the one making the pancakes everybody is obsessed with?" Bella says, skeptical.

"He looks like the waitress," Dee observes, noticing that they share the same round face and swoopy jet-black hair. "Maybe they're brother and sister."

"Mrs. Nelson-Pan mentioned that the kids

help out, the same way the two of you help out at the pharmacy," Ron says. He and Ant are still seated on the other side of the booth, all their attention now focused on the Saturday morning crossword, which they solve together every weekend.

As they wait for their food, the group discusses the big PPS basketball game coming up this Friday. Dee and Eugene want to go—Dee, because Sebastian invited her, and Eugene, because his proximity to the human world via his parents' taxidermy business has always kept him interested in human sports. Bella and Charlie do *not* want to go. They understand basketball about as well as they understand humans, which is to say, they don't get it at all.

While the four friends debate, they all continue to steal glances of the boy in the kitchen as he cooks. He appears to be about their age, and yet his pancakes are the talk of the whole town. What's his secret? At one point, he puts the spatula down and leans in close to the batter.

"What's he doing now?" Charlie says, drawing everyone's attention to the boy again. With their perceptive vampire vision, Charlie can see the pancake batter bubbling furiously on the griddle.

"Maybe it's part of the process," Eugene guesses. "He's gotta be doing something special to make them taste so good, right?"

Suddenly the boy stands upright and hurries out of the kitchen. He runs out from behind the bar and swerves through the crowd to the other side of the diner, where the waitress is carrying a tray of food and milkshakes. At the same time, a little kid tries to move around the waitress by ducking under the tray, but he doesn't quite go low enough. The kid's hat knocks into the edge of the tray, sending it flying out of her hands. But just before it crashes to the floor, the boy from the kitchen drops to the ground and slides on his knees to catch the tray in his arms.

Bella's eyes widen while Dee gasps. Not only did the boy manage to prevent sure disaster, but not even a single drop of syrup was spilled in the process.

The boy stands up and hands the tray back to the waitress. For once she doesn't look annoyed, only a little dazed. "Thanks, bro," she says.

And then, just as quickly as he arrived, he turns on his heel and heads back to the kitchen. Bella and Dee watch him take his post in front of the griddle and resume flipping pancakes like nothing at all has happened.

"Okay." Bella looks around the diner, still packed with crowds and buzzing with chatter. "Did anybody else see that?" She looks at her dads, who still have their eyes cast down over the newspaper.

"Uh, *yeah*. That was wild," Eugene says. "Some parkour moves, if you ask me."

"How did he know the tray was going to fall?" Dee asks. For the first time since they arrived at Scary Good Shakes, she isn't thinking about Beatrice's retirement.

The waitress appears at the end of the booth. Apparently, the tray of food that almost crashed to the floor belongs to them. She passes out the pancakes, the milkshakes, Eugene's breakfast of champions, and finally, Charlie's scrambled eggs with bacon.

Dee immediately takes a sip of her milkshake. Her eyes light up. "It tastes just like Beatrice's recipe!"

"Shocker," Bella says, her voice flat. "Dee, this place is still known for their milkshakes. They're not just going to taste disgusting all of a sudden."

"Yum," Charlie says, looking at their plate of food. They smile so big their fangs poke out. "Nothing quite like a perfectly scrambled egg."

Eugene raises an eyebrow at Charlie. "What about dragon plasma?"

Charlie frowns. "What, you think I can't enjoy human food?" They pick up their fork to take a bite. "Open your mind, Eugene. I contain multitudes."

"NO!"

An arm appears out of nowhere and swats the fork out of Charlie's hand. Bella, Dee, Charlie, and Eugene all look up in surprise. It's the boy from the kitchen.

"Sorry," he says, reaching for Charlie's plate. "But you don't want to eat that. The eggs were cooked in garlic butter. I, uh, think—well, do you maybe have an allergy to garlic?"

"What?" Charlie instinctively leans away from the plate as the boy takes it off the table. "Wow, thanks. I'm super allergic."

"Yeah, I—" the boy starts, but then stops himself. "It's no problem."

"Henry," a voice calls out from kitchen. The boy looks at the window behind the bar, where a dark-haired woman is watching him. "Your pancakes are going to burn!"

"Coming, Mom!" the boy replies. He turns

back to Charlie. "I'll bring you a fresh batch of eggs in just a minute."

He takes off through the crowd again, and all Bella, Dee, Charlie, and Eugene can do is watch him go, feeling more confused than ever.

CHAPTER 2

The rest of the weekend passes uneventfully, so when Bella and Dee get to school on Monday morning, they're still thinking about what happened with the boy at Scary Good Shakes.

"I just don't understand it." Bella zaps open her locker. "How did he know Charlie couldn't eat garlic? They didn't tell the waitress. Do you think the human knows they're a vampire somehow?" Both girls know that would be nearly impossible, though—humans never notice what is sitting right under their noses, including the community of supernatural creatures hiding in plain sight.

Dee removes her notebook from her locker and shrugs. "Maybe Beatrice had something to do with it. She knew all about Charlie's dietary restrictions." She bends over and unzips her book bag to put the notebook inside. Cornelius pokes his furry black head out, meowing excitedly.

"Cornelius!" Dee hurries to hide her book bag in her locker, looking around to make sure nobody else has spotted the cat. "We talked about this! Familiars aren't allowed at school. You'll get us in trouble."

Cornelius widens his big yellow eyes into a pleading sort of pout, and Dee softens. She can never resist that face. "Okay, I guess you can stay. But you have to be *really* quiet."

Cornelius meows his agreement, then ducks back down inside the bag.

Bella shakes her head. "You let him get away with everything." She takes out the books she needs for her morning classes and then zaps her locker closed.

"He'll be good," Dee says, assuring herself just as much as Bella. "But to be on the safe side, let's try to stay away from—"

"Principal Koffin!" Bella says, standing up straight.

"Exactly." Dee hoists her book bag on her back, leaving a little opening at the top for Cornelius, and then shuts her locker the human way. "I don't want to scrub any more cauldrons."

"Bella, Donna," says a familiar stern voice. Dee spins around and comes face-to-torso with Yvette Koffin, the seven-foot-tall harpy principal of YIKESSS. Standing next to her is a goblin woman neither sister has ever seen before.

"Oh, hi, Principal Koffin!" Dee takes a step backward and puts a hand over her shoulder, trying to telepathically communicate to Cornelius that he'd better not move a muscle. "How was your weekend?"

The principal stares at Dee a moment before responding. Though her face gives nothing away, the twins wonder if she already suspects they're hiding something.

"Restful," she says finally. "Thank you for asking." She gestures to the goblin woman standing next to her. "I'd like to introduce you to an old friend of mine, Kathleen Krumplebottom."

Kathleen smiles, revealing sharp teeth—a fashionable trend among mature goblins—and nods a greeting. She's dressed in a fancy suit and has voluminous purple hair. Dee admires the row of gold hoops that line her pointy goblin ears.

"Kathleen is a clairvoyant who has come to YIKESSS to discuss the ins and outs of her psychic abilities in an assembly this afternoon."

Bella's whole face lights up. She's never met a clairvoyant before.

Though anyone in the supernatural community can practice the art of divination, which is using tools such as herbs and cards to predict the future, natural psychic abilities are a rare phenomenon. They can appear in any monster, at any age, without any kind of warning, and tend to present themselves differently in everyone they inhabit. As a result, clairvoyance is the least-understood power in the supernatural community. There is simply no rhyme or reason for why future sight chooses some monsters and not others.

"No way! A real psychic?" Bella lowers her voice, trying to contain her enthusiasm. "Can you tell me if I'm going to be the next Bloody Mary?"

Kathleen shares a private, knowing glance with Principal Koffin, and then says, "Clairvoyance is rarely so specific, I'm afraid. Sight decides when it wants to reveal itself to us, not the other way around."

"Oh." Bella's excitement deflates. "Well, that's not very useful."

"Bella," Principal Koffin warns. "Do try to be polite to our guest."

A look of amusement washes over Kathleen's face. "It's all right, Yvette. Such is the life of a clairvoyant. We spend our days looking for ways to be useful until we drive ourselves mad with all the things we can't change!" She laughs a little maniacally, and then quickly gets serious. "Sadly, some of us don't recover as well as others."

Bella and Dee look at each other warily. Neither twin likes the sound of that.

"I'll go into more detail at the assembly this afternoon," Kathleen says. She glances at Principal Koffin and then leans in closer to Dee. "And keep an eye on your feline around Professor Belinda's raven, hmm? Quite vengeful birds, ravens. One swat and your familiar will have an enemy for life!"

Dee looks up at Principal Koffin, who's now frowning down at her, and smiles innocently. She can feel Cornelius shifting his weight in her book bag.

"I have no idea *what* she's talking about."

Bella and Dee are in the greenhouse, tending to their shrieking sunflowers for Botany class, when the ravens squawk to signal the end of seventh period. Usually the twins would head back to the witch wing for Divination, their final class of the day, but instead they make their way east, to the auditorium where the clairvoyance assembly is being held.

The auditorium and the greenhouse are on opposite ends of the school, so when the twins finally arrive, they look around and discover most of the seats have already been filled.

"I wanted a spot in front," Bella grumbles. She notices Crypta Cauldronson in the front row, right in the center, and glowers.

"Bella, Dee, over here!"

The twins turn their heads to the left, toward the sound of Eugene's voice. He and Charlie saved them two seats in the middle of the auditorium. Dee smiles at her friends and waves. Bella smiles too. At least they won't be stuck in the back.

They scoot through the row, past several classmates, and sit down—Bella next to Eugene, and Dee on the end. Right away they can tell Eugene is nearly bursting with anticipation.

"How wicked is this?" he says to the twins. "We get to meet a goblin psychic!"

Charlie leans around Eugene to look at Bella and Dee. "My mom told me about Kathleen before. She runs a school for psychics, and she works with Creepy Councils all over the world to let them know when trouble is brewing."

"Wow." Bella tucks her hair behind her ear, looking around for Kathleen. "I have *so* many questions."

"Me too." Eugene holds up a notepad and pen from his lap. "Don't worry, I'm going to write down everything. I don't want to forget a word."

"Eugene, I'm impressed," Dee says, leaning over to unzip her book bag. "I don't think I've ever seen you take notes before."

"Well, it's not every day you meet a goblin who decides not to be trickster for a living." He opens his notepad, where the words *Kathleen Krumplebottom, Clairvoyant (and goblin!!!)* are scribbled at the top of the page. "Speaking of, I think I've almost worked out all the kinks in the Tootmaster 6000. Want to help me take it for a test run after school on Wednesday?"

"Can't," Bella says. "I have scream team practice, and then we have to go to something with our dads."

"At a *human's* house," Dee adds, excited.

"Oh." Eugene looks down at his lap. "That's okay, maybe—"

"ACHOO." Charlie sneezes into their arm. "ACHOO. Sorry. I don't know where those came from."

On the floor, Cornelius peeks his head out of Dee's book bag. *"Meow."*

Charlie frowns down at the cat. They reach into the front pocket of their bag and pull out a small bottle of allergy medicine.

"Shh!" Dee looks at Cornelius and holds a finger up to her mouth. "Principal Koffin has ears like a hawk."

The chatter throughout the room starts to die down, and the four friends look up to see Principal Koffin and Kathleen walking to the center of the stage. Bella sits up a little straighter, eager for the assembly to begin. Dee gives Cornelius one more warning look.

"Good afternoon, students," Principal Koffin begins. Her voice is so naturally commanding that she doesn't need to turn on the microphone in front of her. "Today we have a very special visitor here with us, my good friend Kathleen Krumplebottom. Kathleen is a professor and the founder of SEE, the School for Extrasensory Excellence, up in Maine. SEE is a school for studying and harnessing psychic abilities. As a clairvoyant herself, she has graciously agreed to tell you everything you might want to know about her powers."

Bella's hand shoots up in the air. Principal Koffin sees it right away and says, "Hold your questions until the end, please. There will be plenty of time." Bella looks around, realizes she's the only one with her hand up, and then grudgingly lowers it.

"Now, you may be thinking, why must we have an assembly about clairvoyance when we have a whole unit dedicated to it in Divination class next semester? And the answer is simple. I want you to learn about psychic powers from someone who knows them firsthand. As it happens, many of you will probably never meet another clairvoyant in your lifetime." Here she pauses, as a wave of murmurs spreads across the room.

"Clairvoyance is extremely rare," the principal continues. "It's something one is born with, not something that can be taught. And though it can be studied to the best of our abilities, nothing about innate psychic powers can be said with one hundred percent certainty." The principal takes a step back, gesturing for Kathleen to step in front of the microphone. "Kathleen, if you'd like to begin."

Kathleen steps forward and takes a few seconds to lower the microphone to her height. Then she taps it with one long green finger, and the echo booms throughout the auditorium.

"Thank you, Yvette," she says, smiling at her friend. "And hello, YIKESSS! As your principal implied, natural psychic powers are hard to study because there are so many different variables involved. To put it plainly, that means no two clairvoyants are exactly alike in their abilities."

Kathleen takes the microphone off the stand and begins walking back and forth across the stage.

"Some of us experience visions as flashes that burst into our consciousness. Others see visions through objects. And still others can only see the future when the circumstances are right—say, on Wednesdays at noon, and *only* when it's raining. The frequency with which we experience these visions is different as well. Some of us get dozens of visions a day. Others, only one or two a month. And this, too, can change over time. That's why it takes some clairvoyants *years* to realize they have psychic powers at all."

Bella glances at Eugene, who is furiously scribbling in his notebook. He wasn't kidding when he said he didn't want to miss a single word. Bella zaps his pen with a writing spell, and it begins copying Kathleen's lecture on its own. Eugene looks up at Bella, surprised. He gives her a grateful smile.

"You might think it's swell to be psychic—and sometimes it is. You're on your way out the door, about to forget your keys, and then *bam!*" Kathleen yells into the microphone, making several students, including Dee and Charlie, jump out of their seats. "You have a vision of yourself locked out of your house. Now you can grab your keys and avoid a crisis."

"I could've used that one last week," Eugene whispers.

When Kathleen speaks again, her voice is much more somber. "Other times, though, visions of the future can be a real burden. Unwanted and unclear visions are common—more common, in fact, than clear, wanted visions—and often leave their hosts feeling conflicted about how to proceed, which can lead to severe mental strain."

Bella's hand shoots up in the air again. Principal Koffin, who has been hovering at the side of the stage, takes a step forward, presumably to silence Bella, but Kathleen holds out an arm to stop her.

"Yes, Bella Maleficent?"

Bella stands up, unfazed by the fact that every head in the room is now turned in her direction. "What kinds of unwanted visions?"

Kathleen nods, and Bella sits back down. "Every kind you can imagine. Disaster, destruction, fear—even death."

Murmurs sweep across the room again.

"The most important lesson a clairvoyant needs to learn is also the hardest, and it's that no matter how hard they try, they can't control everything. In fact, they can't control *anything*, apart from themselves. As clairvoyants, it's not our job to solve all the world's problems, no matter how badly we may want to. Those who realize this are the ones who will be able to harness their powers successfully. Those who don't, well . . ."

Kathleen stops walking and lets her gaze linger across the crowd. When she's sure she has everyone's attention, she says, "They will make an enemy of their own minds. Some will meet a *terrible* fate."

Without missing a beat, Bella raises her hand again. Dee winces, wishing her sister would stop drawing attention to them and the cat they've smuggled in.

Bella stands up. "Like what *kind* of terrible fate?"

Kathleen hesitates a moment before answering. She looks at Principal Koffin, whose face, as it often does, reveals no emotion. Then she looks at Bella again.

"When I was a young goblin coming to terms with my psychic powers, there weren't many resources available to me. All I had was a friend: a witch named Nina. A vision brought us together, funnily enough. She was clairvoyant too, although unlike me, whose visions come through my thoughts, Nina saw the future in puddles of water.

"I was always just trying to survive, but Nina wanted to help people. Whenever the sight showed either of us something bad, Nina *needed* to fix it. She dedicated years of her life to trying to change the future for the better, and I followed her wherever she went, because I thought it was what I was supposed to do. And then, gradually, I noticed a change in her.

She wasn't sleeping. She became irritable and started to get bad headaches. If she wasn't on a mission to track down a vision, she was staring at puddles of water, waiting for a vision to come. Her obsession with helping other people live better lives made her forget that she had one of her own. Eventually, it made her forget herself completely." She paused. "And it made her forget me."

Bella lets out a small gasp. She looks at Dee, trying to imagine how it would feel to be forgotten by her best friend. Just the idea shrouds Bella's curiosity in a dark cloak of dread. She feels her heartbeat quicken with fear and faces forward, trying to shake off the awful feeling. It's no use thinking about such things. Bella knows her sister would never leave her behind.

In the front row, Crypta Cauldronson raises her hand. "What happened to Nina?"

A distant look passes over Kathleen's face. "Nina passed away, I'm afraid. She interpreted a vision incorrectly, and the cost was her life."

Every student in the room is silent as Kathleen's words sink in. Even Eugene, once giddy with excitement, is now slouched in his seat with a disturbed look on his face.

"I'm not telling you this to scare you," Kathleen says, injecting some energy back into her voice. "Nina's story is a warning, yes, but more importantly, it's a lesson. Clairvoyance is a gift that can be used to help people, but if we're not careful, it can—and *will*—consume us."

She puts the microphone back in its stand and then claps her hands together.

"Now." She smiles. "Who else has questions?"

❧❧❧❧ CHAPTER 3 ☙☙☙☙☙

Over the next couple of days, Kathleen's words weigh heavily on the twins' minds. Bella is frustrated—for all the supernatural community's many advancements, how is it possible there's still so much they don't know about clairvoyants? Surely, she thinks, someone could be doing more research to help the cause.

Dee, meanwhile, is worried—how many clair-voyants must there be, walking around with-out a clue as to what their visions of the future really are? She can't help but think about how confused and alone they must feel.

"We're lucky," Dee says to Bella in their room on Wednesday evening. She sits on her bed with Cornelius curled in her lap, stroking his fur as she speaks. "We've known about our powers since we were babies. We never had to worry about figuring things out on our own because we've always had Dad, Pop, and each other."

"I know." Bella brushes her hair in front of the vanity. "I feel bad for Kathleen. I mean, losing the one person who really understands what you're going through? That must be awful."

"I bet she feels really sad," Dee says, her voice somber. If Bella ever forgot about her the way Nina forgot about Kathleen, well—it goes without saying that Dee would be devastated.

Bella looks at Dee's reflection in the mirror. Her thoughts are an echo of her sister's. "That's never going to happen to us, right?"

Dee blinks in surprise. "Duh. I'd be completely lost without you." From her lap, Cornelius meows in agreement.

Bella gives her sister a small smile, reassured for the moment. "Me too." She puts down the hairbrush and turns to face Dee. "Do you think there are any clairvoyants at YIKESSS?"

Dee shrugs. "If there are, Principal Koffin probably knows about them." She pauses, considering her words. "At least, I really hope so."

"Girls." Ant pokes his head into their room. He's wearing his human makeup. "Ready to go to the meeting?"

Bella stands up. She's still wearing her scream team uniform from practice after school, wanting to show it off to all the humans. "Ready."

Dee tries to lift Cornelius from her lap. He lets out a forlorn meow and wraps his paws around her left leg.

"Sorry, buddy, but you know you can't come," she says. "We'll only be gone a little while."

"I know what will cheer him up," Bella says. She points at a toy mouse in the corner of the room, on top of Cornelius's toy basket, and zaps it with purple sparks. The mouse rises in the air, begins to squeak, and starts moving around the room, dragging a pink tail in its wake. Cornelius's yellow eyes widen. He leaps out of Dee's lap and begins chasing the mouse.

Dee smiles, satisfied. He's so stinkin' cute.

The first thing Bella and Dee notice when they walk into the human living room half an hour later is the color white. White couches, white walls, black-and-white photographs in white frames on a mantel that is coated in white paint.

"I guess it's better than beige," Dee says, taking off her sneakers by the doorway, as she was instructed to do by her dads, so she doesn't track mud on the white carpet.

"White, beige, it's all the same to me," Bella

says. "Boring human decor." She waits until the humans aren't looking and then zaps her boots off her feet and against the wall, next to several other pairs of shoes.

"Antony, Ron, we're so happy you made it," says the woman who answered the door. She has a blond bob and wears white jeans with a gray cardigan. "And you brought your girls!"

Once a month, the PSBS gathers to discuss and strategize how small business owners can work together to best serve their community. This month the group encouraged members to bring their kids and spouses. Bella and Dee have never been to a meeting before, thanks to their unpredictable magic, but since they've been exhibiting a bit more control lately, Ant and Ron decided to test their restraint and bring them along. And the twins were determined to make their dads proud.

"This is Bella and Donna," Ant says, gesturing to each daughter. "Girls, this is Amy Groff. She owns the Happy Hair Salon downtown."

"Hi," the twins say in unison. They look past Amy and see a group of adults—mostly humans—spread out on the couches and chairs that occupy the living room. A vampire who lives one street over from Bella and Dee, and who runs the library, stands in the corner with the least light and nods a familiar greeting in their direction.

"Oh, I just love your little cheerleading uniform," Amy says, and smiles down at Bella. "My Avery cheers too, at PPS. I'm sure you'll have so much to talk about. She's in the kitchen with the other kids."

Bella glances down the hall, toward the kitchen, and frowns.

"Go ahead, girls," Ron said, giving Bella a knowing smile. "Unless you'd rather discuss budget allocations with us."

"Hmm." Bella tilts her head. "Can I think about it?"

"Come on," Dee says, grabbing her sister's arm and pulling her down the hallway.

In the kitchen, Bella and Dee find white cabinets, white countertops, and three other kids seated around the dining table—shockingly not white, but a light oak—munching on an array of snacks. There's a blond girl who looks to be about their age seated in the middle, talking to a kid across from her who can't be more than six years old.

". . . have *got* to stop playing with dolls," she says. "Cool kids don't play with dolls."

"But I love my dolls," the kid replies.

"Well, then you're not going to be cool. Sorry, I don't make the rules."

The kid considers this for a moment, and then shrugs. "My dolls think I'm cool." They pick up a Cheeto from the glass bowl in front of them and pop it in their mouth.

At the end of the table, with all his focus on a handheld video game, a boy with swoopy black hair and a round face slouches into his chair. It only takes Bella and Dee a moment to realize where they've seen him before.

"Hey!" Bella says, and everyone but the boy looks up. "You're the kid from Scary Good Shakes!"

Now he does look up, a confused crease between his brows. When he sees Bella and Dee, something like recognition appears on his face. Then a *bleep-bloop* noise sounds from his video game. He looks back down at his screen and groans. "Shoot. I died."

Bella hurries to take the seat next to the boy. "Okay, you *have* to tell me how you knew Charlie was allergic to garlic. It's been bothering me for days. They hadn't mentioned anything about it in the restaurant, so . . . what's the deal? How did you know?"

"Charlie?" the boy says, looking back down at his game instead of meeting her eyes. "Oh, your friend? I didn't know. I just knew they didn't order it, that's all."

Bella purses her lips, dissatisfied with his answer. And now everyone's eyes are on the girls.

Pushing past her sister's rudeness, Dee says,

"Hi, I'm Dee," adding a little wave for good measure. "And this is my sister, Bella. Our dads own Ant & Ron's. You know, the pharmacy on Main Street?"

"I'm Avery," says the blond girl. "This is Henry and Sam." She locks her eyes on Bella's scream team uniform. "Oh. You two go to YIKESSS?"

Dee nods, trying not to feel bothered by Avery's judgmental tone. She takes the empty seat next to her sister, in front of a veggie platter.

"What's YIKESSS?" asks Sam, mouth full of Cheetos.

"A school for weirdos," Avery replies, as casually as she might have said *a school*, period.

Bella scowls at her. "Excuse me?"

"No offense." Avery picks up a tortilla chip and dips it into some salsa. "That's what my mom says." She puts the chip into her mouth and chews it loudly.

"None taken," Dee says with a genuine smile. "There's nothing wrong with being weird."

"Avery says I'm weird because I play with dolls," Sam tells them, studying the orange Cheeto dust on their fingers. "Maybe I should go to YIKESSS."

"Maybe you should," Dee replies. "I'll put in a good word for you."

Henry looks up from his video game. "Is it true you have to take tests with your feet?"

Dee scrunches up her nose. "What?"

"That's what the kids at PPS say," Henry tells them. "They say a *lot* of wild things about YIKESSS."

Bella rolls her eyes. "That's just a rumor. Some jealous hu—I mean, person probably made it up because they applied and got rejected." She looks across the table. "Hey, Avery, how many times have *you* applied to YIKESSS?"

"Me, apply to YIKESSS?" Avery says, forcing out a laugh. "What a joke. I'd never want to go there in a million years."

"Really?" Henry says. "Then why did you

just send in an application for spring semester?" Henry glances at Bella and Dee with a knowing smile on his face. "Her mom even slid a hundred-dollar bill into the envelope. Not that it's going to make a difference."

Dee covers her mouth with her hands, trying to stifle her laughter.

Avery's jaw drops. "How do *you* know that?"

The boy shrugs. "Just do."

Bella smirks into her lap. It's clear to her now that Avery is no friend of Henry's. For a human, he isn't so bad, after all.

"Whatever, Henry," Avery says. "I've tried to be nice to you since you're the new kid in school, but you know what? You're just as weird as them." She juts her chin out toward Bella and Dee.

"Welcome to the weirdo club!" Dee says to Henry, making him laugh. "We have lots of fun."

"And we have *way* better snacks," Bella says, frowning at the piece of celery in her hand and tossing it back on the table.

"Can I be in the club?" Sam asks. "I'll bring my dolls!"

Avery narrows her eyes at Bella. "I saw you at the fall dance, you know. You had that weird outfit and were dancing with those other two freaks." She eats another chip dipped in salsa. With a full mouth, she says, "I was embarrassed just watching you."

Bella stands up, her hands turning to fists at her sides. "Call my friends freaks one more time."

Dee freezes, glancing from Bella to Avery and back again. She can feel a spark of magic in the air.

"Bella," Dee says, her voice a warning and a salve. It occurs to her, again, how white and pristine everything around them is. How breakable. "Just relax."

"You and your friends . . . ," Avery starts.

"Bella," Dee cuts in, her heart pounding. She can feel the aura of angry magic getting stronger.

Avery doesn't break eye contact with Bella. ". . . are *freaks*."

Dee stands up, ready to jump across the table to snuff out the sparks if she has to. She can't let Bella's magic explode in front of all these humans. Gretchen Cauldronson wouldn't think twice about having their family exiled for much less serious offenses. And the girls can't let their dads down now, after Ant and Ron are finally starting to trust them.

Before Dee can do anything drastic, though, Henry gently touches Bella's wrist with his hand. Bella looks down at him.

Slowly, subtly, he shakes his head. *No.*

The anger drains from Bella's face, confusion taking its place.

"She's not worth it," he says. "Trust me."

Just as quickly as Bella's sparks ignited, they fizzle out. She sits down in her chair, and Dee exhales a breath she didn't realize she was holding.

Avery leans back in her seat, a look of satisfaction on her face. "That's what I thought," she says, and Dee frowns. Avery's arrogance is exactly the kind of stereotype that makes Bella so distrustful of humans.

Henry is frowning too. "You know, Avery, I'd rather be a weirdo with freaks for friends than a bully with no friends."

Dee smiles even though her heart is still racing. Henry stood up for them even though he didn't have to—even though he barely knows them. She decides, right then and there, that she wants to be his friend.

"Ooh!" Sam says, pointing a Cheeto at Avery. "You just got burned."

Bella is still looking curiously at Henry. "Dee," she says, and her gaze shifts to her sister. "I need to talk to you."

Dee follows Bella out of the kitchen and back into the hallway, where the guest bathroom is located. They hurry inside and lock the door behind them.

"Did you see that?" Bella says, eyes sparkling with an idea.

"Yeah," Dee replies, a little disgruntled. "You were two seconds away from casting in front of humans and getting us exiled out of Peculiar." She sits down on the toilet lid and studies the blue shower curtain as her heart rate returns to normal.

"But that didn't happen," Bella says. She hoists herself onto the edge of the counter and sits down, facing Dee. "Because Henry stopped me just in time. It was like he *knew* I was about to cast."

Dee considers this. "I don't think so. Maybe he just thought you were going to dump the bowl of salsa on her or something."

Bella shakes her head—though part of her wishes she would have thought of that in the moment. "First the waitress with the tray, then Charlie with the garlic, and now this. It's all too convenient that Henry always happens to intervene at the right time."

Dee raises her eyebrows. "What are you getting at?"

Bella lowers her voice. "Remember what Kathleen Krumplebottom said during the assembly on Monday? Clairvoyance can appear in anyone. I assumed she meant anyone *supernatural*, but what if humans can get psychic powers too? What if Henry can see the future?"

Dee's eyes widen as Bella's suspicions sink in. "He *did* say that thing about Avery's mom trying to bribe her way into YIKESSS—and how it wouldn't make a difference. *We* know that, since humans will never be allowed to attend YIKESSS, but how could he?"

"Exactly." Bella smiles and shakes her head in disbelief. "Principal Koffin said most of us wouldn't meet another clairvoyant in our lifetimes, and we've already met two in one week. How creepy is that?"

"Let's not get ahead of ourselves," Dee says. "We still don't know for sure that he actually has psychic powers. Either way, that kind of revelation could turn his life upside down."

"Yeah," Bella agrees. "We should know for

sure before we confront him. Otherwise, it wouldn't be just his life that gets turned upside down." She's thinking of the Creepy Council's cardinal rule: don't tell the humans about the supernatural community. Breaking that rule, of course, is punishable by exile, which means asking Henry outright whether he's psychic is out of the question.

"And I don't want to scare him away," Dee says. She picks up a section of green hair and starts anxiously picking at the ends. "I like him."

"Me too," Bella says. "It was really creepy, the way he stood up for us." In her experience, no human has *ever* done that before.

Dee looks up at her sister. "So how do we find out the truth?"

"First," Bella says, "we need a second opinion."

CHAPTER 4

During lunch the next day, Bella and Dee tell Eugene and Charlie about their theory.

"A human psychic?" Eugene takes a big bite of his hamburger. With a full mouth, he says, "I've never heard of that before."

"Well, if he's got psychic powers, he's not technically human, is he?" Charlie points out, looking at their friends behind dark sunglasses. The group is sitting at their usual table by the big window, and the early afternoon sunshine is pouring in. "He's supernatural."

"I knew there was something I liked about him." Bella grins, munching on a carrot from her dad's garden.

Dee nudges her sister. "You liked him when you thought he was just a regular human. And he still *might* be." She looks at Eugene and Charlie. "We don't have any real evidence yet."

"Then we need to get some, right?" Eugene says, taking another bite of his burger. "I mean, we can't just meddle in his life based on an assumption. The last time we tried that, it didn't exactly go so well." He gives Bella and Dee an accusatory look.

Bella frowns in his direction. She knows he's referring to the time they assumed Principal Koffin needed some love in her life—they ended up almost destroying the school. Also, she wishes he'd chew with his mouth closed.

"I get your point," she says. "But it's not like we can just ask him if he's clairvoyant. If we're wrong, we could get in some serious trouble. And he has no idea supernatural creatures even exist. Imagine telling him he might *be* one."

"Plus, we're still on thin ice with Principal Koffin," Dee reminds them. "She already helped us restore the veil. She's not going to want to clean up another mess."

Charlie winces. "I can't get into any more trouble." They pick up their water bottle full of plasma and take a sip. "My stomach hurts just thinking about it."

"And anyway," Bella adds, "if he *is* psychic, he probably doesn't even know it."

"You think?" Eugene says. "It seems like he's getting visions a lot."

Bella shrugs. "Kathleen said it takes some clairvoyants years to figure out they have powers. He doesn't have any monsters in his life to guide him—he probably doesn't understand what's happening."

Eugene picks up a french fry and starts twirling it between his fingers. "A supernatural living among humans, not knowing he's a supernatural." He looks at his friends. "That's pretty huge."

"*If* that's the case," Dee says, her forehead creased with concern, "we have to help him! It must be scary not knowing what he really is."

The group is quiet as they consider this. They've all grown up in the supernatural community, which means they've been aware of their powers—and the responsibility that goes along with them—their entire lives. By not knowing what he's capable of, Henry could unwittingly get himself into some real danger.

"Okay," Bella says. "So without meddling in his life, or doing anything that might accidentally expose the supernatural community, how can we find out for sure if he's psychic?"

"Find out if *who* is psychic?"

The group looks up to find Crypta Cauldronson standing at the end of the table, holding a lunch tray in her hands. Her shiny brown hair has been braided into two buns on the sides of her head.

"No one," Eugene says quickly. He shoves a handful of fries into his mouth.

Crypta narrows her eyes. "I just heard you talking about somebody you think is psychic."

"Psychic? She didn't say *psychic*," Charlie says, forcing laughter. "We said *sidekick*. Didn't we?"

Dee nods, faking laughter alongside Charlie. But Crypta doesn't move. Instead she locks eyes with Bella.

"Tell me."

"Honestly, Crypta," Bella says, resting her elbow on the table and putting her chin in her hand. "Why would we tell you anything?"

"Because if you tell me what you know," she says, "I'll tell you what I know."

This catches all four friends by surprise. They swap uncertain glances. Does Crypta *actually* know something, or is she just pretending to know so the friends will reveal their suspicions?

The last thing they want is for Crypta to find out about Henry and go running to her mom, Gretchen, with the news.

Finally Dee looks at Bella and shrugs as if to say, *why not?* As much as she hates to admit it, Bella sees her sister's point. They were hitting a dead end, anyway.

"Fine," Bella says. "But you can't tell your mom. Promise?"

Crypta smiles, pleased. "Cross my heart and hope to fly." She places her lunch tray on the table and sits down next to Charlie.

"Okay," Bella says. "Yes, we think we *might* know someone who *maybe* has psychic powers, but we're pretty sure he doesn't know."

"Why not?" Crypta picks up her spoon and plunges it into her yogurt. "Wasn't he at the assembly?"

Bella hesitates. She looks at Dee for help.

"He's a human," Dee says. Crypta widens her eyes. "And he's new to town. We just met him a few days ago at Scary Good Shakes."

"That makes sense," Crypta says, nodding.

Charlie furrows their brow. "It does?"

"Yeah." Crypta looks around to make sure nobody is lingering close by. Dee spots Jeanie in the distance, sitting at her usual table in the center of the cafeteria, an empty seat next to her. She's watching Crypta with a confused look on her face.

"My mom told me that Kathleen Krumple-bottom didn't *just* come to YIKESSS to see her old friend Yvette," Crypta says. "She came because she had a vision that there was a clairvoyant in Peculiar who needed her help."

"*What?*" Bella raises her eyebrows.

"But if Kathleen already knows about Hen—" Dee starts, and then backtracks. "About the boy, why didn't she contact him herself?"

"She doesn't know who it is," Crypta explains. "That's why she held the surprise assembly. She hoped it would help the psychic realize their abilities and come forward."

"A good plan in theory," Eugene says.

"Except that the psychic in question wasn't at the assembly."

Crypta nods. "Kathleen told my mom that the vision wasn't clear. All she saw was dark hair, the Peculiar town sign"—she looks at Bella and Dee—"and you two."

Bella grimaces. Dee sinks down in her seat.

"Typical," Charlie says, shaking their head. "Just typical."

"My mom told me to keep my ears open," Crypta says with a shrug. "She said if I overheard anything about who it could be, I should tell her right away. Otherwise, something bad might happen."

"Something bad?" Dee bites her lip, worried. She wonders if maybe they *should* tell Gretchen, after all. But then what would happen to Henry?

Crypta nods. "That's what she said." She eats a spoonful of yogurt, not seeming very worried about her mom's ominous threat. "As soon as they find the psychic, Principal Koffin and Kathleen want to send them away for training immediately, before they can do any damage to themselves or the town."

"Send him away?" Dee says, her concern growing. She doesn't want Henry to get sent away—he just got here. She's hardly even had a chance to get to know him.

"But you're *not* going to tell your mom yet," Bella says, her eyes pointed like daggers in Crypta's direction. "Because we don't want to screw with Henry's life until we know for sure that he's the one. And because you promised. Right?"

Crypta looks at Bella. She sticks out her pinky finger, and yellow sparks shoot from the tip. "I promise."

Bella holds out her pinky and conjures her own yellow sparks. The two girls' magic connects and intertwines, forming a magical pinky promise. If the promise is broken, the witch who goes against their word grows a long Pinocchio nose that can't be zapped away for twenty-four hours.

Once the promise is sealed, Crypta scoots her chair out from the table and stands up. "Keep me updated, 'kay?" She picks up her lunch tray. "And try not to make a total mess of things. If you do, I'm going to pretend I didn't know a thing."

She walks away, and Eugene shakes his head. "Maleficent, what are you thinking? You just made a deal with the devil."

"Worse," Charlie says. "With Crypta."

"I'm *thinking* that our hunch is right, and Henry has psychic powers." Bella looks around at her friends. "Who's up for a late-night stakeout at Scary Good Shakes?"

"You know me," Eugene says. "When mischief calls, I always answer."

"I'd prefer to let it go to voice mail," Charlie says. "But I'll come too."

They all look at Dee. Despite her worry about what could go wrong, she thinks it might be worse for Henry if they do nothing. It's one of their more noble efforts, as far as schemes go. Plus, there will surely be strawberry milkshakes involved.

"Okay." She nods. "I'm in."

~~~~~~~~ CHAPTER 5 ~~~~~~~~

After checking in with their dads, Bella and Dee meet Charlie and Eugene at Scary Good Shakes at seven thirty, half an hour before closing time. It's not very busy—only a few tables are occupied—and a sign by the host station tells them to seat themselves. They decide on the booth with the best view of the kitchen.

"There he is," Dee whispers. She can only see the back of him, but there's no mistaking his messy black hair as he stands in front of the griddle, flipping pancakes. "Try to act natural."

"Hi there!" A cheery middle-aged woman appears with a stack of laminated menu booklets and passes them out. It's Henry's mom. Bella and Dee recognize her from the kitchen on Saturday and the small business owners meeting yesterday. "Can I start you off with something to drink?"

Dee doesn't hesitate. "A strawberry milkshake, please."

The others in the group give their milkshake orders, and then Bella says, "Can we also get a stack of pancakes for the table?"

"A big stack," Eugene says, though he just came from dinner with his parents. "The bigger, the better."

Bella raises her brow. "Your stomach is a bottomless grave."

"Hey." He shrugs. "You're buying, I'm eating."

When the woman takes their order to the kitchen, the friends prop the menus up and use them to create a barrier to talk behind.

"So, what are we looking for, exactly?" Charlie asks, careful to keep their voice down.

"Evidence," Eugene says.

Charlie's mouth forms a straight line. "Thanks, Count Obvious. I meant what *kind*? Do we just wait until he has a vision?"

"Let's think about this," Dee says. "The last time we were here, he was flipping pancakes one minute and catching that falling tray the next. Same for when he stopped Charlie from eating the garlic."

Bella picks up a section of hair and starts twirling it around her finger, thinking back to Monday's assembly. "Kathleen said visions of the future aren't always in the mind. Sometimes they appear externally, in other objects."

"Like her friend seeing the future in puddles of water," Eugene says.

Bella nods. She peeks over the top of her

menu at Henry, who's still standing over the griddle in the kitchen. "I wonder if his visions are connected to the diner somehow."

Charlie reaches into their bag and pulls out a small leather book. There are no words written on the front. "I checked this out from the library after school. There were no textbooks on clairvoyance, but I did find this diary." They open it up to the first page. "It belonged to a vampire who lived in the early 1900s. From what I've read so far, it seems like they kept a log of every vision they ever had."

"Gnarly," Eugene says. "I can barely remember to write down my homework."

"The vampire's visions were activated by heat," Charlie continues. "You know when it's hot outside, and you see the little squiggles coming off the pavement? That triggered their visions. So did stoves, ovens, steam from hot baths—"

"Shh!" Bella snaps.

Henry's mom appears with a tray carrying

four milkshakes. "Now, what's going on here?" She gestures to the menus with a giggle. "Having a top secret meeting?"

"Oh, just doing some homework." Dee grins as her strawberry shake gets placed in front of her. "Thanks so much!"

The woman looks at Bella and Dee. "You two are Antony and Ron's girls, right?" Dee nods, and the woman smiles wide. "Oh, they're just the best. They've been so welcoming to us as we've gotten settled in." She finishes handing out the milkshakes and says, "I'll let you get back to it. That homework isn't going to do itself!"

"Not yet, anyway," Bella mutters. She's pretty sure her dads have that spell locked away in the Cabinet of Doom, the filing cabinet in Ant and Ron's study that is strictly off-limits to the twins.

When the woman is safely out of earshot, Bella leans behind the menus and whispers, "So what's your point, Charlie? You think Henry's visions are activated by heat too?"

"Not just heat," Charlie says, taking one long slurp of their vanilla shake. "*Pancakes* and heat."

Dee widens her eyes. "You mean, like, he sees the future in pancake batter?" She smiles. "That's awesome."

Charlie nods excitedly. "My theory is, the pancake batter hits the griddle and starts to bubble up, and that's what triggers the visions."

"That's a pretty specific way to see the future," Eugene says skeptically. His milkshake glass is already half-empty. "Maybe too much of a reach?"

Bella tilts her head, considering. "Kathleen *did* say no two clairvoyants have the same psychic powers. That means some powers would have to be pretty specific. Right?"

"Right," Charlie agrees. "Plus, it might not be the only way he gets visions. Just the most reliable way."

"Okay, okay. I see your points," Eugene says. "But how do we prove it?"

"Hey."

All four friends jump in their seats and look up over the menus. Henry is standing at the end of the table, holding a plateful of pancakes and looking at them curiously. "What are you doing?"

"Nothing," Dee says quickly, then takes a long sip of her milkshake. "Mm, tasty!"

Bella shoots her sister a look, then hurries to knock down the menus now that their cover is blown. "How did you know we were here?" she asks him. "Did you . . . have a feeling?"

"Uh." He raises an eyebrow. "No? My mom told me." He looks around the table, and his gaze rests on Eugene. "You okay? You look kind of green."

"Thanks!" Eugene smiles. "I've been getting a lot of sun lately."

Henry puts the plate of pancakes in the center of the table. He didn't skimp on the stack— there have to be a couple dozen pancakes there. "Here you go. I have to say, I think this is a first.

Nobody has ever ordered a stack of pancakes for the table before."

"We really love pancakes," Dee says. She scoots farther into the booth. "Can you take a break and sit with us?"

Henry glances around the diner. At this point it's almost closing time. There are two other tables still occupied, but both look like they're ready to pay the check.

"Okay, sure," he says. "I can sit for a few minutes." He takes a seat at the end of the table next to Dee.

"You're Henry, right?" Eugene says, piling pancakes on his plate. Henry nods. "I'm Eugene, and this is Charlie."

Charlie smiles and waves over their milkshake. "I use 'they, them' pronouns, by the way."

"Cool." Henry smiles back. "It's nice to meet you both."

"Hey, Henry." Eugene lowers his voice. "Where's that waitress who was here on Saturday?"

Bella rolls her eyes.

"My sister?" Henry makes a face. "Who knows. She hates working at the diner. She's still pretty mad at my parents for moving us here." He hesitates. "And me, for being the reason we had to move."

Bella leans in eagerly. Gathering evidence in favor of Henry's psychic powers just might be easier than they thought.

"Where did you move from?" Dee takes a big sip of her milkshake. She grimaces. "Ow, brain freeze."

"Just outside Philadelphia." Henry leans back in the booth and puts his hands in his sweatshirt pockets. "My parents used to run a restaurant in the city."

"Is that how you learned to cook so young?" Bella asks.

"Yeah," Henry says. "Food has always been a big part of our family. My mom's Korean, and my dad is from the South, and they loved incorporating food from both their families into the menu. I'd hang out in the kitchen after school and help them come up with cool new recipes."

"Oh, *man*," Eugene says, chewing on a pancake doused in syrup. "These pancakes are *delicious*. Seriously." He swallows and takes another big bite. "They're so good, it's like magic."

Bella bites the inside of her cheek to keep from laughing at the irony. Then it dawns on her: maybe magic really *is* the secret ingredient.

"People back home used to say that too," Henry says, smiling down bashfully into his lap. "My pancakes were the most popular thing on the menu."

"I'm not surprised." Eugene finishes the pancake in three bites, then moves onto the next one.

"But if the restaurant back home was doing so well," Bella says, a curious crease forming between her eyebrows, "why'd they move here and buy Scary Good Shakes?"

The smile fades from Henry's face. "I was sort of having a not-great time in school. The other kids, they . . . you know. They didn't get me." He shrugs.

"What?" The expression on Dee's face is one of disbelief. "But you're awesome."

Henry looks at Dee. "They didn't think so. And things only got worse after I started spending all my free time at the restaurant."

"What do you mean?" Bella asks, leaning forward. "Worse how?"

Henry seems uncertain. "I don't really know how to explain it. It was like . . . like I couldn't ever pay attention. Teachers and other kids would try to talk to me, and my mind was always somewhere else. The only place I could ever *really* feel calm was cooking in the kitchen."

Bella and Dee share a glance.

"My parents thought maybe it was stress related," Henry says. "That's why they moved us to Peculiar—for a fresh start."

"And has it been?" Charlie asks, finishing their pancake. "A fresh start?"

Henry runs a hand through his messy black hair. "Honestly? It's just more of the same. I'm still having trouble focusing, and the kids at school are . . ." Here Henry looks at Bella and Dee. "Well, you both met Avery Groff."

"Unfortunately," Bella scoffs.

Henry sighs. "I have to make it work here. I already put my family through so much with the move and making them give up the restaurant. I don't want to give them any more to worry about."

Dee frowns. She feels sorry for Henry. If he really is a clairvoyant, no number of fresh starts will fix his problems with concentration and feeling like an outsider. In fact, according to Kathleen's lecture, if he doesn't learn how to manage his visions properly, all this will seem like nothing compared to the bad stuff that could happen down the road.

Then Dee remembers Crypta's warning. When Principal Koffin and Kathleen find the clairvoyant, they're going to send whoever they are away for training. That means Henry's fresh start in Peculiar would be over before it even began.

Dee looks at her sister and knows they are both thinking the same thing. They have to help Henry. But how can they do it without uprooting his life *again*?

"Well, things will be different now," Dee says, giving Henry an encouraging smile. "Because you have us."

"Yeah. Consider this your official fresh start," Bella adds, raising her milkshake in the air. "Welcome to Club Weirdo."

"Club Weirdo?" Eugene says, though his mouth is so full of pancakes you can hardly make out his words. "That sounds wicked. I want in."

"You already *are* in." Bella nudges him. "We all are."

"To Club Weirdo," Charlie says, raising their fork in the air and clinking it against Bella's milkshake. The others follow their lead.

"Thanks," Henry says after they all clink. He looks down. "Honestly, I've never had a real group of friends before. I don't really know what it's like." He looks up and around the table. "Do you have sleepovers?"

"Oh, *do* we," Eugene says. "Last weekend we had a pizza-making contest and a movie marathon." He raises his brow at Henry. "Do you like *Space Wars*?"

Henry shrugs. "Sci-fi is okay. But what I really like"—he reaches into his pocket and pulls out a deck of cards—"is magic."

Dee's jaw drops. Does Henry know more about the supernatural community than he's letting on?

"Magic?" Bella says, just as shocked as Dee. "You can do magic?"

In one fluid motion, he fans the cards out and places them in front of Dee. "Pick a card."

Dee looks around warily at her friends before choosing the card right in the middle. She has no idea what to expect.

"You can look at it," Henry says. "But don't tell me what it is. Once you've memorized it, put it back in the deck."

Dee looks at her card—the two of hearts—and shows it to Bella, who's peering over her shoulder. Then Dee puts the card back in the deck.

All four friends watch, fascinated, as Henry thoroughly shuffles the deck. His movements are quick and precise, indicating to the twins that this is something he's done many times before. Finally he stops shuffling. He places the pile of cards down in front of Dee and pulls the first one off the top.

"Is *this* your card?" He flips the card over onto the table, revealing the two of hearts. Dee gasps in delight.

"Wow!" Dee claps her hands together. "That was amazing!"

Bella is a little more skeptical. "How did you know that?"

Henry smiles into his lap. "It's nothing. Just a little magic trick."

Bella's mouth widens in surprise. "Why didn't you tell us you know divination?"

Henry gives her a strange look.

"A magic *trick*, Maleficent," Eugene says. "Some humans—I mean, *people*—like to pretend to do magic. They're called magicians." He looks eagerly around the table. "One time, I saw one pull a rabbit out of a hat."

Bella scrunches up her nose. "What's so magical about a rabbit in a hat?"

Henry gathers the cards and puts them back in his pocket. "I'm not a magician or anything," he explains. "I can only do a few card tricks. But I do think magic is super cool." He sighs. "I wish it was real."

Bella, Dee, Charlie, and Eugene all look at each other. Nobody says a word.

~~~~~ **CHAPTER 6** ~~~~~

The next morning is fraught with indecision as Bella, Dee, and their friends go back and forth over what to do about Henry. While last night's stakeout gave them some clarity— namely, that Henry is probably psychic—it didn't make their decision about what to do next any easier. If Henry does have psychic powers, and they say nothing to Principal Koffin about their suspicions, they could be putting him in danger. But if they tell her, Henry will have to leave Peculiar, and he can kiss his fresh start—and their newfound friendship—goodbye. And that's assuming their theory is true. If Henry isn't actually psychic and Principal Koffin finds out they were meddling unnecessarily in her business again, they will probably get in big trouble. The girls are still on thin ice after what happened last time, when they almost destroyed the school, exposed the supernatural community, and got their principal taken away to the Underworld. Bella and Dee don't want to make a mistake like that again.

As Bella and Dee are on their way to lunch, still arguing about what to do, they're intercepted by Argus the four-eyed crow, holding a letter between his talons. It's addressed to Bella and Dee, written in Principal Koffin's telltale cursive handwriting. Bella takes it from Argus and rips it open as the bird flies away.

"Principal Koffin wants us to stop by her office for tea," Bella says, her eyes skimming the words. "Right now."

"Now?" Dee's eyes go wide with worry. "You don't think the birds heard us talking about Henry, do you?"

"I'm not sure." Bella lowers her voice and looks around. They tried to be discreet in their conversations, but the campus birds are like Principal Koffin's spies, always on the lookout for fresh gossip to bring her.

They turn around and head back in the direction they came from, making their way to Principal Koffin's tower office. When they get to the entrance at the bottom of the stairs, Bella says, "Remember, keep as quiet as a corpse. Don't say anything about Henry unless Principal Koffin brings him up first."

Dee nods in agreement.

They take their time moving up the winding staircase, not making a sound until they get to the top and use the brass knocker to announce their arrival. The door swings open on its own.

"Come in, girls," Principal Koffin says. She's not seated at her desk, where they usually find her, but in an antique chair in the corner of the room, next to a small, circular table. On the table are three teacups sitting atop matching saucers, decorated with a delicate floral pattern. The girls can see the steam rising from the hot tea.

"Take a seat," the principal says. Argus, resting on his perch, watches the twins' every step as they cross the room and sit down on the bench by Principal Koffin's desk.

"Would you like some green tea?" the principal asks. "I find it a divine way to relax when I'm feeling tense."

"Tense?" Bella laughs nervously. "We're not tense."

"Definitely not," Dee says, picking at her cuticles.

The principal tilts her head an inch to the

left. "I never said you were." She pauses. "So, no tea, then?"

Bella, who hates tea, looks at Dee. Normally Dee wouldn't hesitate to say yes, but today she's afraid her hands will shake if she tries to hold on to the cup and saucer.

"Um, okay," Dee says. As usual, her desire not to be perceived as rude trumps her fear. "I'll take some."

Principal Koffin stands up and brings her a cup. As Dee take the tea, she silently begs her hands to remain still. They don't obey. She quickly puts the cup and saucer down on the bench next to her.

"I'm glad you were both able to see me today," the principal says, returning to her seat. Her face, usually so stoic and composed, shows a trace of worry. This doesn't help Bella's and Dee's nerves at all. "I haven't had a chance to check in with you since the restoration of the veil."

Surprise crosses Bella's face. "The veil?" She

looks at Dee, who shares her confusion. Neither of them expected that.

Principal Koffin nods. "I've been worried about how you two have been getting on. What happened was quite . . . intense. Certainly a lot for two young witches to handle." She pauses to take a sip of tea. "I just want to make sure you're both doing all right."

"Oh." Bella exhales a sigh of relief. "No worries, Principal Koffin. We're doing just fine." She smiles. "Is that all?"

Principal Koffin turns her gaze to Dee, who's looking out the window, letting her tea get cold. Even though it's not the incident with the veil that's got her worried, Dee can't quite get behind her sister's assurance that everything is fine. She prefers looking out the window to meeting the principal's eye.

Principal Koffin stirs her spoon in her teacup. "You know, if something is bothering you—not just today, but anytime—I want you to feel comfortable confiding in me." She puts the spoon down on the table. "My door is open whenever you want to talk."

Dee turns away from the window. She picks up her tea and takes a sip. Her hands are no longer shaking, but she can still feel her heart beating quickly in her chest.

"Donna." The principal is watching her. "Is something on your mind?"

"No, not at all," Bella answers for her. "She's just upset because she messed up a charm in Spell Casting today. Right, Dee?" She makes a pleading face in her sister's direction and mouths the word "corpse."

Dee looks at Argus the crow, whose all-knowing eyes seem to bore right through her. She sighs. "It's just . . . We thought we were doing the right thing when we brewed that love potion. We wanted to help you, and we ended up making everything worse."

Principal Koffin nods, encouraging Dee to continue. Bella bites her lip, unsure what's about to come out of her sister's mouth.

"I guess I've been wondering. If you think someone you care about is in trouble, how do you know when it's your place to help them and when you should stay out of it?"

Dee takes another sip of her tea, now lukewarm. Bella sits back in her seat. It was a good question, she has to admit.

For a few moments Principal Koffin doesn't reply, just picks up her spoon and swirls it through the liquid in her cup again. "There's no right answer to your question, I'm afraid. What it really comes down to is intuition."

Bella raises her brow. "What do you mean, intuition?"

"Your gut feeling about the situation," the principal explains. "You have to weigh all the factors and decide for yourself if getting involved is going to make things better or worse."

Bella crosses her arms. She and her sister have been doing that all day and are still no closer to coming up with a decision.

"But what if your intuition is wrong?" Dee presses. "I mean, how can you ever really trust yourself to know the decision you're making is the right one?"

"You can't." Principal Koffin sips her tea. "The only thing you can know for sure is that your intentions are pure. Whether you choose to help or not, whatever happens as a result of your decision is out of your hands."

Bella shakes her head. "That's not good enough. What if you do nothing, and something bad happens? Or someone gets hurt?"

Principal Koffin takes one final sip of her tea and puts the cup down on the table. "Even if things don't go the way you want them to, you can find solace in the knowledge that you did what you thought was best."

Dee looks down at her feet. "It's frustrating," she says, "having all this power and still feeling so helpless."

Principal Koffin smiles sadly. "In time, it will get easier to trust yourself. You still have so much to learn—about your powers *and* yourselves. And as you grow in your abilities, so, too, will your confidence grow."

Suddenly Argus caws and flaps his wings on his perch, making Dee jump and spill some tea on her uniform skirt.

"Ah," the principal says. "That will be my twelve thirty lunch meeting with Vice Principal Archaic."

Bella perks up. "*Lunch* with Vice Principal Archaic? Ooh la la."

The look Principal Koffin gives Bella next could curl even Bloody Mary's toes.

The twins leave the principal's office feeling possibly even more conflicted than when they arrived.

"Maybe we should have told her about Henry," Dee says, walking behind Bella down the winding staircase.

"And get him sent away right when he's starting to feel like he belongs?" Bella says. "No way. Club Weirdo sticks together."

"I don't want Henry to leave either," Dee says. "But what if it's the best thing for him? *We* don't know anything about clairvoyance."

"Speak for yourself," Bella says. "You know I'm a fast reader."

Dee feels a buzz in her blazer pocket. She pulls out her eyephone, waits for the eye to open, and looks at the screen. "It's a group text from Henry. He's inviting us to the diner after hours tonight to try a new pancake recipe."

Bella unzips the front pouch of her book bag and takes out her eyephone. She immediately fires off a response in the new group chat, aptly named *Club Weirdo*: YES! Just have to make sure it's ok with our dads

Dee purses her lips, thinking of Sebastian. "But we were thinking about going to the PPS basketball game tonight."

"*You* were thinking that," Bella says. "I was thinking of faking my own disappearance."

Bella's and Dee's phones buzz with more incoming messages.

Eugene: A new recipe? OMG!!

Eugene: Henry, u should try pancakes with slugtruffles. Would totally enhance the flavor

Charlie immediately texts Eugene in a separate chat with just Bella and Dee, one they made after the first day of school, called *The Ghouls*.

Charlie: NO, EUGENE!

Charlie: Humans don't have slugtruffles

Eugene: Oh my b

Bella and Dee both laugh. Their phones buzz again. It's Eugene, back in the Club Weirdo chat:

Eugene: Nvm

Eugene: They're European

Eugene: Got any strawberries?

~~~~~ CHAPTER 7 ~~~~~

When Bella, Dee, Charlie, and Eugene get to Scary Good Shakes, it's half past eight in the evening, and the new moon is high in the sky. The front door is locked, and it's freezing outside, so Bella knocks aggressively on the glass until she sees Henry's familiar swoop of dark hair coming out of the kitchen, moving toward them. As soon as he gets close enough that she can see his face, Bella frowns.

"Something's wrong. Henry doesn't look too good."

Dee, Eugene, and Charlie all shove Bella out of the way to get a better look. She's right: Henry seems paler than usual, and he's got a grimace on his face like he's in pain. He unlocks the door and gives them all a weak smile. "Hey."

The four friends file into the diner one by one. "I'm happy you're all here," Henry says, and then locks the door behind them. Bella and Dee both notice the way he keeps his eyes down, away from the lights.

"Are you all right?" Bella asks without missing a beat. "You look terrible."

"Not *terrible*," Dee corrects her sister, unzipping her green coat. "Just a little sick, maybe."

"Oh." Henry runs a hand through his hair. "I'm fine. My head just hurts a little." He winces. "Or a lot."

"You have a headache?" Bella says, taking off her hat and looking meaningfully at Dee. They learned during Kathleen's assembly that headaches are a symptom of uncontrolled psychic abilities.

"I get them sometimes," Henry says, squinting at the ground. "It's no big deal."

The friends all look at each other. Nobody seems very convinced.

"Maybe you should sit down." Dee puts her coat on a table by the door and takes a step toward him. "We can get you some water."

Henry seems to hesitate. "Okay. I'll sit for just a minute. I don't want the pancakes to get cold." Dee heads to the kitchen for a glass of water while Henry sits down in the nearest booth and slumps forward, resting his head in his arms. When he speaks again, his voice is muffled. "Sorry about this. I'm probably just dehydrated from standing over the griddle for so long."

"Don't be sorry," Eugene says, sliding into

the booth across from him. "Do you get head-aches a lot?"

Henry lifts his head a little, propping his chin in his hand. "I used to get them only once in a while. But lately, they seem to be coming more and more."

"That's awful," Bella says. She puts her jacket and beanie on the same table as Dee's coat, and then sits down next to Henry. "Have you been to a healer?"

"She means a doctor," Charlie corrects her, sliding in next to Eugene. Bella waves away the mistake with a flick of her wrist.

Dee returns from the kitchen with a glass of water and places it on the table in front of Henry, then sits down next to Bella. Henry smiles gratefully as he picks up the glass—a movement that appears to cause him even more pain.

"Yeah," he says, and takes a sip of water. "Like three different ones. They run their tests, tell me everything looks normal, and then give me medicine and send me on my way." He pauses to take another sip. "It doesn't help, though. Nothing does. The headaches come out of nowhere and then . . ." He trails off. He blinks a couple of times and sits up straighter. "It's gone. Huh."

"Just like that?" Dee says. She notices that Henry already looks more energized. Some of the color is returning to his cheeks. "Your headache is gone?"

Henry nods. "It's strange. And it only started a couple of minutes before you got here."

"The same thing happened to the *character* in this *book* I read," Charlie says, raising their brow suggestively at their friends. Of course, Bella and Dee both know what *book* Charlie is referring to—the diary of the vampire with psychic powers they picked up from the library. "They got these headaches that would be really intense for a few minutes, and then they'd disappear like nothing ever happened."

"Yeah, that's exactly what it's like," Henry says. "What's the book called? Maybe I'll read it."

"Oh, um . . ." Charlie glances around. "It's called *Diary*. But you can't read it. It's . . ." Their gaze settles on Eugene. "It's European! I read it when I was on vacation with my mom in Italy."

"Oh, okay," Henry says. He turns his head toward the kitchen, and Eugene gives Charlie a subtle thumbs-up. "Wait here. I'll go get the pancakes from the kitchen."

Dee and Bella stand up to let Henry slide out of the booth, and then they sit back down. As soon as he's out of earshot, Bella says, "So I think it's safe to say that Henry is clairvoyant. Right?"

"Definitely," Charlie replies, their voice low. Next to them, Eugene nods in agreement.

"He said his headache started right before we got here," Dee reminds the others. "That was probably when he was cooking the pancake batter." She puts her elbows on the table. "I wonder what kind of vision he had."

"Poor guy." Eugene's ears droop a little. "He just wants to cook his pancakes and do his magic tricks in peace."

"Maybe he still can," Bella says. "He can live a normal life if he learns how to control his visions."

"Who's ready for some cookie dough crunch cakes?" Henry says, returning from the kitchen with two plates stacked full of pancakes. He sets them down in the middle of the table. "Pancakes with chunks of cookie dough and potato chips baked inside, and then drizzled in fudge. I hope they're still hot."

Eugene's ears perk up again, and his eyes nearly bulge out of their sockets in excitement. "Oh, hex yeah. Let me at 'em." He starts shoveling pancakes onto his plate.

"These pancakes are my way of saying thank you," Henry says, looking around the table. "You've all been so nice to me. My whole life, other kids have made me feel like an outsider, but you never made me feel that way. Right away you accepted me for who I am, and I can't tell you how much that means to me."

"Of course we did," Bella says. "We're all

weirdos here. It's so much more exciting than being normal and boring. Don't you think?"

"Yeah." Henry grins. "I do now."

"I'll eat to that," Eugene says with a full mouth.

Dee smiles, but her heart isn't in it. She's too worried about Henry—about the secret they're keeping from him—to feel very hungry.

The pancakes are delicious, and fortunately, Henry doesn't get another headache during the meal. Together, the five friends have no trouble clearing both plates—thanks in large part to Eugene—and even make themselves a round of milkshakes for dessert (strawberry for Dee, of course). After some serious urging by Eugene to put cookie dough crunch cakes on the menu, plus another one of Henry's card trick demonstrations, to the twins' delight, Bella, Dee, Charlie, and Eugene are ready to head back home. They put on their coats, hug Henry goodbye, thank him once more for the pancakes, and tell him they'll see him soon.

They wait until they leave the diner and are halfway down the block before anyone dares to speak.

"It's official. We have to tell Principal Koffin," Dee says, crossing her arms as she walks. The temperature has dropped even more since they were last outside, and a light snow has begun to fall. "Even if it means Henry has to leave Peculiar for training. It's the only way to help him."

"Maybe he doesn't have to go away," Bella says, her voice hopeful. She squints at her friends through the snowflakes. "Charlie, what did the vampire in the diary do to get rid of their headaches?"

"They tried a lot of different things," Charlie says. "But it seems like the only thing that really worked was not giving in to their visions. The more they let their clairvoyance control their life, the worse the headaches got."

Bella nods. It's just like what Kathleen said during the assembly. "Well, Henry can't control his visions if he doesn't even know what they are." She looks around at her friends. "Some-body has to tell him he's clairvoyant."

"Not me," Charlie says immediately. "Con-frontation gives me hives."

"It shouldn't be any of us," Dee insists. "It should be Principal Koffin."

Eugene doesn't look convinced. "I don't know. Wouldn't it be less scary if the news came from one of his friends, instead of, you know, a seven-foot-tall harpy?"

Dee shakes her head. "She's been around for hundreds of years and has probably met every kind of supernatural creature there is. She'll know how to handle it better than us."

They get to the end of the street and stop at the crosswalk, waiting for the walk signal to light up. The bus back to Eerie Estates is on the next block.

Bella sighs. "Dee's right. We should tell her." All three friends turn to look at Bella, shocked. This might be the first time she has ever agreed to get an adult involved in a crisis.

"What?" she snaps at them. "I want what's best for Henry too. Even if it means he has to go away. Jeepers creepers, can't a witch learn from her mistakes?"

"Totally," Eugene says. "I just wasn't sure if *you* could."

Bella snorts. She holds her hand out flat, palm facing the sky, and conjures a snowball in a burst of white sparks. Before Eugene has time to react, she throws it at him, and it hits him in the chest.

"Hey, no fair!" Eugene dusts himself off. "You can't bring magic to a snowball fight."

"Oh yeah?" Bella smirks, conjuring another snowball. "Watch me!"

She throws this one at him too, but he ducks just in time. The snowball whizzes past Eugene and collides with someone else, who until that moment has been lurking just out of sight.

Dee recognizes him first. She wonders how long he's been listening.

"Henry?"

Bella, Eugene, and Charlie freeze as they all

watch Henry step out of the shadows and into the dim light of a streetlamp. He has Bella's hat in his hand and a stunned expression on his face.

"How—how did you just do that with the snow?" Henry says, his eyes darting between them all. "And what do you mean I'm 'clairvoyant'?"

"Whoops," Eugene says. "Guess the cat's out of the cauldron."

"And you two—" He points at the twins. "Witches and supernatural creatures? What are you *talking* about?"

Dee takes a step toward him. "We can explain everything."

But Henry takes a step back, the shock on his face giving way to anger. "You've been lying to me this whole time." He takes a few more steps back. "I told you things I've never told anyone. I thought we were friends."

"We are friends!" Bella says. "Just *wait*. The feelings you've been having, the headaches you've been getting—there's a reason for all of it. We just wanted to make sure it was true before we—"

"No!" Henry drops Bella's hat on the snowy concrete and puts his hands over his ears. "I don't want to hear any more! I—*agh*." Henry leans over, his hands moving to his temples. He's getting another psychic headache.

"Henry, I know you're scared, but come with us," Charlie says. "We're on your side."

Henry shakes his head. "I'm not going anywhere with you." He takes a few more steps back. "You want to send me away!"

"We don't!" Dee says. "We want to help you!"

"No!"

Henry turns around and starts running in the opposite direction.

"Henry," Dee calls out. "Wait!"

"We try to do the right thing and it totally backfires," Bella mutters. "What else is new?" She picks up her hat, dusts off the snow, and pulls it down over her head.

"Well, what are we waiting for?" She looks back at her friends. "Let's go get him."

~·»»»~ **CHAPTER 8** ~«««·~

All four friends take off down Main Street. Bella, Dee, and Eugene run after Henry on foot, while Charlie transforms into a bat and flies high up in the sky.

"Can you see him?" Bella yells up to Charlie, pumping her legs as fast as she can.

"Uh-huh," Bat Charlie replies. "He made a

left on Strange Street and cut through the play-ground. It looks like he's heading right for the PPS gym."

"Oh no." Dee groans. As much as she wanted to go to the PPS basketball game tonight, it's probably the worst possible place for Henry to have a meltdown about supernatural beings. All those humans packed into one room! Not to mention the fact that Sebastian will be there—how is she supposed to be funny and charming in the middle of such a huge crisis?

"We have to run faster if we want to reach him before he gets inside!" Bella says. She and Dee pick up their pace while Eugene huffs and puffs behind them.

"If I had known we were going to be run-ning," he says, "I wouldn't have eaten so many pancakes!"

"If *I* had known," Dee replies, "I wouldn't have left my broom at home."

They follow Henry's path down Strange Street, across the playground, and through the field that PPS uses for football practice. When they arrive at the edge of the gymnasium parking lot, they find Henry hunched over in the middle of a row of cars, trying to catch his breath.

"Henry!" Bella calls out, and he turns his head toward the sound of her voice. At the same time, Bat Charlie appears behind Bella and transforms back into their mortal form.

"AH!" Henry sees the transformation and takes off running toward the gymnasium doors. Dee frowns at Charlie, while Bella turns around and gives them her best Bloody Mary glare.

"I'm sorry, I'm sorry! Jeez," Charlie says, covering their eyes with their hands. "Stop looking at me like that."

The group hurries to catch up to Henry, but he's too far away. By the time they get to the middle of the parking lot, where he *was*, Henry is swinging open the gymnasium doors and disappearing inside. Bella, knowing they could lose him in the crowd, stops running, braces herself, and then, using all the concentration she can muster, beams to the doorway, leaving Dee, Charlie, and Eugene behind in the parking lot.

"Whoa," Eugene says. "Now *that* was wicked."

Dee says nothing, but an uneasy expression crosses her face. Beaming, or zapping oneself from one location to another, is an advanced form of witch travel. Only Level 5 witches are allowed to practice it at YIKESSS, and even then, they're taught to proceed with extreme caution. Inexperienced beaming is very dangerous. If Bella isn't careful, she could wind up beaming to someplace she never meant to go, or worse, get herself stuck in the In-Between—a dimension for lost witches. But Bella, as usual, is impatient to unlock the full scope of her powers. When Dee has tried to discourage her, it's only made Bella more firm in her resolve to be the youngest witch ever to master beaming.

Bella stands in the doorway, propping the door open with her foot and keeping an eye on

Henry. "He's going under the bleachers," she calls out to her friends.

When Dee, Charlie, and Eugene catch up to Bella, she says, "We should split up. Dee, Eugene, you two go around to the other side. I'll stay over here with Charlie. We can try to corner Henry under the bleachers."

"You got it, boss," Eugene says with a salute.

Dee scrunches up her nose. "What makes her the boss?"

"I'm the oldest," Bella says, like it's simple. "Now hurry!"

Bella and Charlie move toward the home-team bleachers, where Henry went, and Dee and Eugene walk under the away-team bleachers to cross the gym unseen. It's not a hard thing to do—commotion fills the room. It's a rivalry basketball game, so the stands are packed. Both teams have cheerleading squads pumping up the crowds from the sidelines, each one fighting to be the loudest and most school-spirited. Bella recognizes Avery Groff in the middle of the PPS squad and sneers in her direction.

Under the bleachers, Bella and Charlie spot Henry right away. He's sitting on the ground, probably hoping he can remain there without being spotted until the game ends. When he sees Bella and Charlie, he stands up.

"Henry, please don't run away!" Bella says, as the crowd above erupts into cheers and applause. The PPS Porcupines must have scored. "I know it's a lot to take in, but you have to trust us."

"Club Weirdo has to stick together!" Charlie adds.

"Trust you?" Anger and betrayal are still written all over Henry's face. "Why would I trust you with anything *ever* again?"

Because we know what you're really going through, Bella wants to say. *Because we care about you.* But before she gets the chance, Henry turns in the opposite direction and runs away from them again. Fortunately, Dee and Eugene appear at the other end of the bleachers just in time, blocking Henry's path.

"Please, Henry." Dee struggles to keep her voice calm over the swell of the crowd above them. "Just wait a minute."

Henry stops in his tracks, looking back and forth between the friends, frantically trying to map out his next move. When it becomes clear that he's not going to be able to get past them, Bella and Dee each let out an exhale. Their plan worked: the chase is over.

And then Henry jumps up, grabbing onto the bleachers above him and hoisting himself up through the space between the bench and the walkway.

"No!" Dee screams, but her voice gets drowned out by the cheers that sound from the crowd above them. Another basket for the Porcupines, and the chase is on again.

Bella follows Henry's lead and climbs up through the bleachers right where she stands. Dee, who knows she's much too clumsy to carry out such a maneuver, runs out from under the bleachers and climbs on in front—the old-fashioned way. Charlie and Eugene do the same, but on the other side.

Bella pulls herself through the bleachers and stands upright, startling the two humans on either side of her. She scans the crowd for Henry and finds him running down the middle aisle. "Dee!" She points at Henry, and her sister spots him. Dee hurries to meet him at the bottom of the stairs. When Henry sees her, though, he turns around and starts running up the aisle.

Dee takes off after him, knowing he'll get to the top and have nowhere to go. She motions for Charlie and Eugene to blockade the other aisles, so Henry has no choice but to run into one of them when he comes back down.

On the floor, the cheerleaders signal the crowd to start doing the wave. The people around Dee stand up and raise their arms, and the wave ripples across the bleachers. Henry, seeing this as an opportunity for escape, ducks into a row and follows the wave all the way down to the next aisle. By the time Dee realizes where he's gone, the crowd is sitting again, making it harder for her to move past them.

"Excuse me," she says, hurrying in front of people as fast as she can, trying her best not to trip over anyone's feet. "Sorry, sorry. I'm—oh! Sorry for stepping on your popcorn. Excuse me."

"Dee?" says a voice she'd know anywhere. Hearing it makes the bats in her stomach flutter their wings.

She looks up. Sebastian is sitting in the row behind the one she's currently shuffling through, wearing his PPS Porcupines hat. She stops moving and smiles. "Hi, Sebastian."

"I'm happy you made it," he says, scooting to the left. "I wasn't sure if you were coming, but I saved you a seat just in case."

"Really, you did?" She feels her cheeks heat up and hopes he can't tell. "That's so nice."

"Henry!" Dee hears Bella say.

Dee turns her head to find Henry two aisles

over, running down the stairs past Charlie. Eugene tries to block his path at the bottom of the aisle, but Henry spins around, faking Eugene out and narrowly slipping by him. Henry jumps out of the stands and lands on the gym floor, then takes off again.

"Well?" Sebastian looks at Dee curiously. "Do you want to sit down? You can have some of my nachos."

For a moment, Dee thinks about saying yes. She looks back at Henry, who's running to the opposite side of the gym with Charlie and Eugene trailing behind him. What if he never stops running? If he doesn't want their help, they can't force it on him. Dee could throw in the towel right now, sit down, and have a great time with Sebastian.

She frowns. Even as she's thinking it, she knows it's a fantasy. She wouldn't be able to have a great time, with Sebastian or anyone, knowing her friend is hurting.

"I wish I could," Dee says. "But my friend is

in trouble, and I have to help him. That's why I'm here."

"Oh." Sebastian's smile falls just a little, and it nearly cracks Dee's heart in half. "That's all right. We can hang out another time. I hope your friend is okay."

Dee smiles gratefully. "Me too."

Another round of the wave comes, giving Dee a chance to move easily through the rest of the row and get to the next aisle. She sees Bella standing on the bottom step and hurries to get to her.

"I'm here!" Dee says. Bella doesn't reply. She's focusing intensely on the basketball game. "What are you—"

Dee sees sparks out of the corner of her eye and looks down at Bella's hands, which she holds close to her stomach. One hand is casting, and she's using the other like a shield to block her sparks from view. The crowd around them lets out a collective gasp as the ball slips out of a PPS player's hand and bounces to the other side of the court. Across the gym, the away-team bleachers erupt with whoos and cheers.

"—doing?" Dee finishes.

"Henry is over there, using the basketball team to hide from Charlie and Eugene," Bella explains. "I had to get the ball to the other side of the room so they could get to him."

As she speaks, Dee watches Charlie and Eugene cross the court, hurrying to catch up to Henry. Henry, of course, sees them coming. He runs down the court, in front of the away-team cheerleaders, and crosses back over to the home-team side. The away team gets control of the ball and brings it back to the center of the court, blocking Eugene and Charlie once again.

"Do it again!" Dee says to Bella, and Dee jumps down from the bleachers to try and stop Henry from running. Bella zaps the ball to the opposite side of the room again, causing another ripple of gasps through the crowd, giving the ball back to PPS and allowing Eugene and Charlie enough time to cross back over.

A referee blows the whistle at Eugene and Charlie. She points angrily at the sidelines, signaling for them to get off the court. A section of the away-team crowd starts booing them, while the PPS crowd, who must think they're a diversion intended to trip up the away team, cheers them on.

Dee comes face-to-face with Henry in front of the PPS cheerleaders, who are in the middle of constructing their pyramid. She notices, with some distain, that Avery is being hoisted to the top. When Henry sees Dee, he swerves to the right, about to cut in front of the pyramid, but rethinks his route when he sees Eugene and Charlie coming that way. He cuts behind the cheerleaders instead, and Eugene tries to intercept him, but Henry gets away just in time. Eugene trips over Charlie's foot and falls into the base of the pyramid, sending Avery and all the other cheerleaders crashing down into one big pile on the floor.

Eugene, who has experienced much harder falls than this one, jumps right back up and smooths down his shirt. "My bad!" he says to the cheerleaders, and then resumes chasing after Henry.

Eugene, Dee, and Charlie follow Henry off the basketball court and into what turns out to be the away team's locker room. The lights are dimmed, and the only sound is the distant chatter of the crowd coming from the gym. The room, thankfully, is empty.

Bella arrives a few moments after everyone else. When she gets there, she finds Dee, Eugene, and Charlie standing over Henry, who's sitting on a bench with his head in his hands. It seems they've finally tired him out.

"Fine," he says, refusing to meet any of their eyes. "Let's talk."

CHAPTER 9

A crackling fire glows beneath the mantel in the Maleficent living room, setting a serene scene for Henry as he sits on the couch between Bella and Dee. Eugene and Charlie sit across from them, sharing a blanket on the love seat in front of the window. Through the glass, they can see the snow as it drifts gently down from the sky and settles into an even layer of white on the ground.

"So witches are real," Henry says, staring into the fire.

"Yep," Dee responds, stroking Cornelius's back as he rests in her lap.

"And vampires, goblins, ghosts, unicorns—all the magical creatures we read about in fairy tales. Those are real?"

"Pretty much," Bella says, munching on a chocolate chip cookie.

"Not unicorns," Eugene says, reaching for the popcorn bowl on the coffee table. "At least, I don't *think* so. I've never seen one."

Ant emerges from the kitchen, carrying three mugs of hot chocolate. "Eugene, have you ever taken a trip to the forests of Indonesia?"

Eugene shakes his head as Ant puts the hot chocolates on the coffee table. Ron walks into the room behind him, carrying two more mugs and a bag of mini marshmallows.

"Then it makes sense that you've never seen

one," Ron says. "They're very shy, and they don't show up on camera."

Henry picks up one of the mugs. "I thought that was vampires."

Charlie sighs and shakes their head. "Henry, you've got a lot to learn."

Suddenly the gold-rimmed mirror hanging above the mantel glows blue around the edges.

"That must be Yvette," Ron says. The first thing the Maleficents did when they got back to the house was call Principal Koffin to update her on the night's events. Of course, she insisted on speaking to Henry immediately. Since she's under the protection of the veil to hide from Hades and her sisters, and therefore can't leave YIKESSS to come to the house, they all decided the magic mirror was the best way to get through to him.

Ron approaches the mirror so it can scan his face. A moment later his reflection is replaced with Principal Koffin, framed by a view of her office.

"A magic mirror?" Henry widens his eyes. "What, do you have, like, a cauldron in the kitchen too?"

"Actually"—Bella sprinkles marshmallows into her mug—"our cauldrons are in our room."

"We can show you if you want!" Dee adds.

Henry grimaces. "That's okay. Another time."

"Ah, hello, Mr. Maleficent," Yvette says to Ron, and then looks off to the side. "Kathleen, I've gotten through to them." Yvette scoots a little to the left. Kathleen Krumplebottom's voluminous purple hair and the tips of her green ears appear in the frame.

"Hello there!"

"A little higher, Kathleen," Ron says. "We can't see you."

Kathleen's hair disappears for a moment. They can hear some rustling, followed by the sound of furniture being dragged across the room.

"Mind the floors, please, Kathleen," Yvette

says to her. "I just had them waxed." Then the back of a chair appears in the frame, followed by Kathleen's face.

"Is that better?" She leans in close to the mirror. "I'm standing on a chair."

"Perfect," Ron says. He steps off to the side, and Kathleen smiles at everyone in the room. "Hello, kids! Is this our clairvoyant, here, in the middle?"

"His name is Henry," Bella says, a little defensively.

"Henry, of course," she says. "I'm Kathleen. It's so lovely to meet you. I've been looking everywhere for you, you know."

"You have?" Henry says. As much as he tries to hide it, the twins can see how scared he really is. "Why?"

"Because I have psychic abilities, just the same as you, and I had a vision that you needed some guidance."

Henry raises his brow. "You mean, you see the future in pancake batter too?"

Kathleen laughs. "No, no. My visions come to me a little differently. In fact, every clairvoyant has their own unique method of accessing their gift."

"Gift," Henry repeats with a snort. "Getting random visions of bad things that are going to happen isn't a gift." He looks down at the mug in his hands. "It's a curse."

"Oh, you poor dear," Kathleen says, her forehead creased with sympathy. "I know how frightened you must be. You didn't ask for this—of course you didn't—but what you will learn, in time, is that clairvoyance is not all bad. In fact, you're seeing good things too. *Helpful* things. You've just been so consumed by the bad that you haven't been paying attention."

"Really?" Henry looks up, still skeptical, but for the first time since he learned the truth about his powers, there's a little glimmer of hope in his eyes too. "But how do you know that? I can't think of a single time I saw something good."

"Because, my dear boy, I've been where you are. It might come as a surprise, but I haven't always been this cool, collected goblin you see before you." Kathleen shares a private, amused glance with Principal Koffin. "I was quite consumed by fear for many years—fear that something bad would happen, fear that I wouldn't be able to stop it, fear that I felt like it was my *responsibility* to stop it. Fear was all I could see!"

Henry nods. Kathleen's words seem to be resonating with him even more than Bella and Dee realized they would.

"Tell me," Kathleen says, "have you been getting headaches?"

"Yeah," Henry says. "Bad ones. They make me dizzy sometimes."

"That's what we call a psychic migraine," Kathleen says. "Very common among young clairvoyants especially, as they're the ones who have the least amount of control over their powers."

"So you mean, if I learn to control my . . . powers"—Henry makes a face like he's in disbelief at his own words—"the headaches will stop?"

"Indeed they will," Kathleen says. "The headaches happen because your subconscious wants to push your visions out of your mind. But visions, as you'll learn, cannot be forced away. No matter how hard you try."

Henry doesn't say anything, just looks down at the floor and lets his black hair fall over his eyes. It seems this bit of information is the hardest for him to hear.

"So the visions will never stop," he says. "I'm going to have to deal with this forever." It's a statement, not a question.

Kathleen doesn't respond right away, and a heavy silence hangs over the room. Finally, Principal Koffin is the one to speak up.

"Yes, you'll be psychic forever," she says. "The same way all of us in this room must deal with our supernatural traits, which will forever ostracize us from the rest of humanity. We can choose to give in to despair that we are different, or we can learn to live with our abilities as best we can. And then, one day, we might even come to find that we love them, because they make us who we are."

Bella and Dee swap a glance. They know Principal Koffin is speaking from experience, though they've never heard her talk like this before.

"I know it feels like you're carrying the weight of the world on your shoulders right now," the principal continues. "But it doesn't have to be that way. If you let us, we can help make the weight lighter. We can make you *happier*."

"It's true," Dee says. She rests a comforting hand on Henry's shoulder. "We're all here for you, and we'll do whatever we can to help you."

"But why?" Henry looks at her. "Why do you want to help me so badly?" She notices his dark eyes are welling with tears.

"Because you're one of us," Bella says simply. "Maybe you've been having such a hard time because you haven't had anyone who really understands what you're going through. But we do. And we're not going anywhere."

"We meant it before, when we said we were your friends," Charlie adds.

"You're in Club Weirdo now." Eugene puts down his mug of hot chocolate. "You don't have to feel alone ever again."

With that, Henry smiles, letting them know their words of assurance are stronger than all the uncertainty he was harboring inside. He's *not* alone, and things *can* get better. Finally he realizes it.

"Okay." He wipes a tear from his cheek and then looks at Principal Koffin and Kathleen. "So, what do I have to do now?"

CHAPTER 10

It's a cold Saturday afternoon in Peculiar, Pennsylvania, and Bella, Dee, Charlie, and Eugene are throwing Henry a going-away party next to the lake in Moonlight Park. Despite the frost that clings to the grass around them, and the layer of ice on the lake, the friends are soaking up the sun in T-shirts and shorts. A warm-weather spell hangs like a spotlight over their picnic blanket, turning the harsh winter wind into a salty ocean breeze. Thanks to the unpleasant chill in the air, they have the place to themselves and are free to relax away from the prying eyes of any curious humans.

"Now this is the kind of magic I could get used to," Henry says, closing his eyes and raising his face toward the sun.

"Me too." Eugene licks an orange Popsicle. "You witches are really starting to get the hang of your powers."

"Don't look at me." Bella's eyes are hidden behind a pair of heart-shaped sunglasses. "This one was all Dee. She's got a knack for nature spells." She licks her cherry Popsicle, which is the same shade of red as her sunglasses.

Dee blushes, smiling into her lap. "I wanted Henry's last day in town to be extra special."

At the reminder that Henry has to leave soon, everyone's sunny dispositions dim just a little.

One week has passed since the conversation about Henry's powers in the Maleficents' living room. Since then, a lot has changed. Kathleen explained that it would be best for Henry if he went with her to SEE for a little while. At SEE, he can learn to control his psychic powers and harness his full potential as a clairvoyant. And since Kathleen is the headmaster, she'll be able to watch over him and make sure he's okay—a condition that Bella and Dee absolutely *insisted* on.

"I'm really going to miss you all," Henry says, fiddling with a balloon string instead of meeting their eyes. "I know we only met a couple of weeks ago, but it feels like I've known you all my whole life."

"Oh!" Dee leans forward and throws her arms around Henry. "We're going to miss you so much!"

"The next few months are going to feel like *forever*," Bella whines.

"But we'll still talk all the time," Charlie says, applying a fresh layer of Sunscream to their face. "Now that you're a supernatural, you *have* to get an eyephone so we can all eyechat."

"Definitely," Henry says. "And you'll look after my parents while I'm gone, right? I know they'll worry."

For Henry, the hardest part of this whole process is not being able to tell his parents the truth about where he's going, or anything about his powers at all. But as Principal Koffin explained, letting humans in on their secret is a dangerous game. She says it will be better for everyone if Henry's parents think he was accepted, on full scholarship, into a prestigious culinary school up in Maine. Though Henry hates to lie to his parents, he knows it's better than the alternative—his family getting exiled from Peculiar for revealing the existence of supernatural beings. He already made them uproot their lives once.

"Of course we will," Dee says. "And our dads will too."

"You know we'll be at Scary Good Shakes,

like, every day," Eugene adds. "Though it won't be the same without your pancakes." His ears droop a little.

"By the way," Henry says to Eugene. "As of this morning, cookie dough crunch cakes are officially on the menu." He grins. "Consider it my going-away present."

"Really?" Eugene's ears perk right back up. "You're the best!"

"We have a going-away present for you, too," Bella tells Henry. She reaches behind her and reveals a small black box tied with sparkly silver ribbon.

"Wow." Henry takes the box. "You didn't have to." He unties the ribbon and opens the lid, and his whole face lights up.

"A deck of cards!" He pulls the deck out of the box. The cards are shiny and black, and at first they appear to be blank. When he picks the top one off the pile and examines it more closely, ink appears. It's a moving image of Dee with a crown on her head, zapping hearts into each corner with red sparks. Then she looks out of the card and waves at Henry.

"They're infused with magic," Bella says. "Forget kings, queens, jacks, and aces. Now you've got Bellas, Dees, Charlies, and Eugenes."

Henry puts the cards back in the box and hugs the whole thing to his chest. "This is really special," he says, and all four friends can hear the emotion in his voice. "Thank you so much."

A burst of blue sparks to their left catches the group by surprise. They turn their heads to find Kathleen standing there, holding the handlebars of a strange-looking silver bicycle with two seats.

"No way!" Bella widens her eyes in excitement. "A beam bike? Those are super rare."

"You didn't think we were going to walk all the way to SEE, did you?" Kathleen smiles. Beam bikes are transportation devices imbued with witch's magic so other supernatural creatures can beam from place to place. In order to get her hands on one, Kathleen would've had to pass a series of rigorous tests. "I'm sorry to break up the party, kids. But it's time for me to take Henry home so he can pack up his things and say goodbye to his family. Then we will be on our merry way!"

Dee's eyes immediately fill with tears. She waits for Henry to gather his belongings and hoist his bag onto his back. Then she hugs him again. "Text us when you get there."

"And don't leave out any details about your trip on the beam bike," Eugene adds, hugging Henry after Dee. "I've always wanted to ride one."

"We'll see you in the spring," Bella says, next in line for a hug. Her sunglasses hide her tears, but her sniffles give her away. "By then, I just know you're going to be the most powerful psychic *ever*."

Charlie is the last to hug Henry. "I'm so glad we met you," they say, squeezing tight. Henry holds on to Charlie the longest. When he finally lets go, he has a strange look on his face.

"I know it's sad to say goodbye," Kathleen says. "But it's only for a short while. And when you return, you'll be a happier, healthier version of yourself."

Henry still seems uncertain. He steps off the picnic blanket, moving toward Kathleen, then gets hit with the cold and starts to shiver. He stops walking and turns back to face his friends.

Dee frowns, sensing something isn't right. "What's wrong, Henry?"

Henry looks at Kathleen. "I'm not sure. . . ." He looks back at his friends. "I think . . . I think I just saw something."

"What do you mean?" Bella says. "A vision?"

"Fascinating," Kathleen says. "Your visions are already evolving."

"I saw a castle," Henry recalls. "And a banshee woman, running away from someone. It looked like she was afraid." He furrows his brow like he's trying to remember. "She was speaking Spanish, so I couldn't understand most of what she said. . . . There was just one word I could make out."

Here, Henry looks directly at Charlie. "She said your name."

Charlie's face goes blank with fear. "Mom?"

Henry nods.

"I'm sorry, Charlie," he says, a grave look on his face. "But I think your mom is in trouble."